ISBN 0-448-40066-9

90000

9 780448 400662

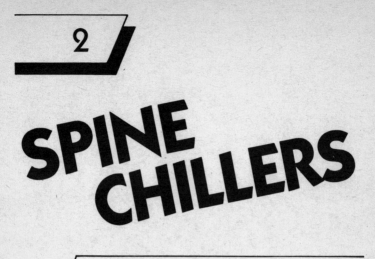

2

SPINE CHILLERS

CREATURE FEATURE
AND OTHER TALES OF HORROR

BY JIM RAZZI

Cover illustration by Jacqueline Rogers
Illustrated by Karin Kretschmann

PUBLISHERS • Grosset & Dunlap • NEW YORK

Contents

The Last Stop

"I'LL HAVE TWO slices of pizza with extra cheese and garlic," Jason told Sal. "And an orange soda, please."

Jason watched as Sal sprinkled the cheese and garlic on the slices.

"They'll be ready in a minute," Sal said as he put them into a huge oven.

Jason's friends Chuck and Tony had already taken their pizza to a table in the back. They were both having theirs plain.

As Jason waited for his order, he looked up at the large clock on the wall behind Sal. It said three-fifteen.

On any other school day, Jason would be on the school bus, going home. But Jason had talked his mother into letting him go with his buddies to Sal's Pizza Palace.

Jason's family lived just outside of town. He never got to meet his friends after school. "How about if we make Friday pizza day?" he had asked his mom. "I don't have any homework. And I can take the town bus home." The last stop was only a short walk from his house.

"Well, okay," his mom had said. "But be sure you catch the four o'clock bus. It gets dark early this time of year."

Jason looked out the front window of Sal's. It was still light. But since it was late in November, he knew the sun would be gone in an hour.

Sal handed Jason his food. Jason juggled the pizza and the soda and went to join his friends. Chuck and Tony were already busy eating.

When Jason sat down, Chuck said, "I almost forgot. I got a new comic book."

Chuck reached into the side pocket of his parka and pulled out a rolled-up comic. The boys all leaned over the table while they ate. They took turns reading the different characters' lines. And they joked around a lot. Jason forgot about the time.

All of a sudden he jumped up from his seat. "Oh, no!" Jason cried. "It's five after four. I've missed my bus. My mom's going to kill me."

"So take the next bus," said Tony.

"The next bus is at four-thirty," Jason answered. "And the ride takes half an hour. It'll be dark before I get home."

"Well, what are you going to do?" asked Chuck.

Jason shrugged. "I guess I'll take the four-thirty bus. But I bet it will be a long time before my mom lets me stay in town after school again."

Jason left his friends and went to the bus stop to wait for his bus. The sun had started to set. And now a cold wind was blowing. Jason shivered and hunched down into his blue ski jacket.

He was happy to see a bunch of people also waiting for the bus. He hoped one or two would be getting off at his stop. But as he looked down the line, he didn't see anyone he knew.

He shivered again and looked for his bus. But it was nowhere to be seen. Jason and the others just waited and waited. He heard the woman next to him say impatiently, "The bus is twenty minutes late."

"Just my luck," said a man next to her. "Now

I'm going to miss the five o'clock news on TV. I always watch it."

Jason looked up. The sky was dark now. His mother was really going to kill him.

Just when he thought he couldn't take the waiting any longer, he saw the bus coming down the street. A few seconds later, it stopped in front of him.

Jason sighed in relief. Well, at least he would soon be on his way.

He bounded up the steps of the bus and put his money in the coin box. He was just about to take a seat when he noticed the bus driver looking at him.

This was the strangest-looking guy he had ever seen. His black hair was combed straight back from his forehead. And his skin looked very pale, as if he never saw the sun.

But the weirdest part about the driver was his eyes. They were dark and angry-looking and seemed to stare right through him.

The driver gave Jason a closed-mouth grin. Then he said in a strange deep voice, "Nice night, isn't it?"

Nice night? Jason thought, shaking off a shiver that was climbing up his back. It was cold and damp and windy. It certainly wasn't *his* idea of a nice night. But he didn't spend more time thinking about it because the people behind him were pushing him forward.

Jason went to the middle of the bus and sat in a seat by the window. He watched the other people get on.

The man who had said he was going to miss the news got on. He looked at the driver and said in a loud voice, "Where's Pete?"

"Pete?" the driver said. Jason could hear him from where he was.

"Yes," the man answered. "The guy who drives the four-thirty bus. I take it every night."

The driver nodded and said smoothly, "Oh, Pete. Of course. He's on vacation. I'm filling in for him. This is my first night on the job."

The man nodded back and said, "Oh." Then he took a seat up front.

"How come this bus is so late?" the man asked. "Pete is always on time. I'm going to miss my news show."

"I can only work at night," the driver answered. "I couldn't get down to the station any earlier."

What the driver said made sense to Jason at first. But then he wondered if the bus company would keep someone on the job who was late his first time.

When all the passengers were finally on board, the bus pulled away. It bumped along the road that led out of town. Jason settled down in his seat. He was suddenly tired.

Nearly a half hour later Jason quickly opened his eyes. He realized that he must have been asleep. He saw that there were only three other passengers left on the bus.

He looked out the window to see where they were. He recognized an old church they were passing.

Good, he thought. It was only a mile to his stop.

But the bus made another stop first, and the other three riders stood up to get off. For one crazy second Jason almost got off with them. He suddenly didn't want to be alone with the strange driver.

But he stayed in his seat as the bus started up again and headed for the last stop.

Half a mile down the road, the driver swerved into a side road. Jason felt his heart jump in his chest. This wasn't the way home. Besides, he knew there were no houses down this way. The road came to a dead end in some woods.

"Hey!" he cried out in a hoarse voice. "Where are you going?"

The man kept on driving.

Jason was about to get up from his seat when the bus stopped with a lurch. They had come to the dead end.

Now the driver slowly turned around. As the man stared at him with those strange eyes, Jason felt stuck to his seat.

"Hey," Jason said again. But this time it sounded like a whimper.

Then the driver stood up and came toward him. He didn't seem to be walking as much as *gliding*. And his eyes had taken on a red glow, as if they were lit from behind by tiny bulbs.

When the driver was no more than a few feet away from Jason, he smiled. Among the even white teeth were two huge sets of fangs. He said, "We're all alone now, my young friend."

With a shudder Jason suddenly realized what was facing him. He had seen enough horror movies and read enough horror comics to know the truth.

The driver had said he worked only at night. He had a dead-looking face and red glowing eyes. He had fangs. The driver was a vampire!

"Yes, my young friend," the man suddenly hissed. "I see you know the truth. I am a vampire."

"Why—why me?" was all that Jason could stutter.

The vampire shrugged.

"I was waiting to get *one* of you alone," he said. "So why not you? It's your bad luck that you were the only one going to the last stop."

Jason cringed in his seat as the vampire glided nearer. His mind raced, trying to remember all the things he knew about vampires. Things he had learned from books and movies.

Drive a stake through his heart? Jason doubted he could do that even if he had a stake.

Shove a cross in his face? Jason didn't have a cross.

But maybe I can make one with my fingers, he thought. He saw that in a movie once and it worked. And there was something else he knew about vampires. He couldn't quite remember what it was. But it was something that drove them crazy.

Now the vampire was almost upon him. Jason leapt out of his seat and ran to the back of the bus. He wanted to put off the end until the very last minute.

The vampire only smiled. Those long white fangs looked sharper than ever.

"Why fight it, my young friend?" said the vampire. Once more he came toward Jason. "It will be all over in a few seconds."

Jason made a cross with his fingers and cried, "Be gone!"

The vampire just laughed in his face.

"That works only in the movies," he sneered.

Then the horrible creature bent over until his face was only inches from Jason's. His eyes stared at Jason's neck.

All at once Jason screamed at the top of his lungs. "Help! Help! Help!"

The vampire reeled back as if Jason had punched him.

Holding his hands over his nose, the night creature ran out of the bus with a howl and disappeared into the night.

Jason stood with his mouth open and his breath coming in short gasps. Suddenly he could smell his own breath. It smelled of *garlic*!

That was the thing he couldn't remember. In the books he'd read and movies he'd seen, vampires could not stand the smell of garlic. It drove them crazy. One of the ways to keep a vampire away was to wear a wreath of garlic around your neck.

Jason smiled. He had saved himself by getting extra garlic on his pizza!

Jason got off the now-empty bus and headed for home. He was sure he had nothing more to fear from the vampire that night. All he had to worry about now was facing his mother.

Gargoyle in the Garden

DEREK STOOD IN his uncle's garden, staring up at the life-sized statue that loomed above him. It was a strange creature with huge outstretched wings. It had long claws on its hands and feet. Its long spiky tail was curled around its muscular, hairy-looking body.

Although Derek knew it was only a statue, the face frightened him. It had evil-looking eyes, a low forehead, and a long, beaked nose. And its mouth was wide open, as if in the middle of a scream.

"It's a gargoyle," said a voice behind Derek. He turned away from the statue and saw his uncle Tobias.

Derek was staying with him for the weekend. Uncle Tobias was very rich and had traveled all over the world. Along the way he had collected many strange things.

Derek thought that his large house, out in the country, was wonderful. There were spears and blowguns and handmade clothes and rugs. There were scary masks and all kinds of statues.

Uncle Tobias was proudest of the statues. He had built a large garden on the land behind the house. Statues stood beautifully among bushes, large trees, and bright flower beds. Tobias had sent Derek out to look at his newest statues.

"What's a gargoyle?" Derek asked as he turned back toward the frightening creature.

"Gargoyles are carved figures that buildings used to have hundreds of years ago. They were placed along roof gutters to carry away rain water." Uncle Tobias pointed to the statue. "There's a hole in the back. Water would pour through there and come out the mouth."

"Did everyone have gargoyles on their roofs, Uncle Tobias?" asked Derek.

"No," answered his uncle. "Only large buildings such as cathedrals and castles used to have them. As a matter of fact, this one came from the castle of an old wizard."

"Do you think it's magical?"

Uncle Tobias laughed.

"Well I don't know about that," he said. "But I guess the wizard thought so."

"Why?" asked Derek.

Uncle Tobias pointed to a sentence in Latin that was carved around the body of the gargoyle.

"It says here, 'THE FIRE FROM THE SKY WILL LIGHT THE SPARK OF LIFE.'"

"What does that mean?" asked Derek.

Uncle Tobias looked at the statue for a minute.

The gargoyle seemed to be looking back at them with a sneer on its frozen face. Derek lowered his eyes with a shudder. He thought he saw the creature's mouth move.

"I really don't know," his uncle answered. "But I wouldn't worry about it."

He hit the statue with his hand.

"It's just a piece of stone, after all."

Derek nodded and turned away. The gargoyle gave him the creeps. He didn't want to look at it anymore.

Then he saw another statue thirty feet away.

"What's that one over there?" Derek asked, pointing to it.

"Ah, that's my newest statue, and my favorite,"

his uncle answered. "It's the goddess of the hunt. It came from the ruins of an ancient city that was known for its statues and magic."

Derek walked toward the goddess. His uncle trailed behind.

The goddess was wearing a short dress. One arm was pulling back the string of her bow. An arrow was held by the string.

"I had to have a new bowstring and arrow made," Uncle Tobias explained as he came up. "Those parts were missing when the statue was found."

"She's beautiful," Derek said in wonder.

Uncle Tobias smiled and agreed, "That she is, my boy. That she is."

As they stood there looking at the statue, a sudden wind blew up. Uncle Tobias looked at the sky.

"I think we're in for a storm tonight," he said. "I can smell it in the air. With this heat, it could even be a thunderstorm."

That evening, when Derek was getting ready for bed, he wondered if it really would storm. He loved thunderstorms. Both his room and his uncle's, next door, had a pair of large glass doors that opened onto the garden.

Derek stood at the doors of his room in his pajamas. He looked out onto the garden. Small spotlights lit up the statues. He could see the goddess clearly. She looked ghostly pale in the light.

The gargoyle was hidden by a row of bushes. That was just as well.

Derek decided to leave the blinds on the doors open. That way he would be less likely to miss the storm.

A loud crash of thunder woke Derek up with a start. He looked around sleepily for a minute. Then he remembered where he was. He looked at the clock near his bed. It was four in the morning.

There was a sudden flash of lightning. Derek put on his slippers and went over to the doors. He opened them. No rain had fallen yet. Derek went outside to get a better look at the storm.

A rush of wind banged the doors shut behind him. Derek jumped at the noise. But then he shrugged and headed toward the statue of the beautiful archer. As he passed a row of bushes, the gargoyle came into view. In the dark night, the creature looked almost alive. Derek suddenly decided he could see enough of the storm from his bedroom.

But before he got inside, a bolt of lightning zigzagged down from the sky. It hit the gargoyle. Derek jumped back as the statue crashed to the ground. As he stared at the fallen gargoyle, he saw it move. But that couldn't happen, he told himself.

Then under the lights Derek saw the gargoyle move again. He backed away, horrified, unable to take his eyes off the statue. Suddenly he tripped over a rock. With his arms windmilling, he fell on his back.

He hurried to his feet with a small cry. At that second, he thought he saw the gargoyle get to its knees.

He couldn't believe his eyes. It must have been a trick of the light, he thought. Still, he couldn't wait to get out of there.

But as he turned to run, he felt as if he couldn't move a muscle.

Derek looked over his shoulder. He saw the gargoyle get up from the ground! He suddenly remembered the words, "THE FIRE FROM THE SKY WILL LIGHT THE SPARK OF LIFE."

Could it be true? Could the magician who had owned this statue have put a spell on it?

Even in his fright, he understood that the *fire from the sky* was lightning! And now that the statue had been hit, the *spark of life* had been lighted.

Another flash of lightning struck the garden. Derek saw the gargoyle standing on its back legs, sniffing the air like a strange bear. There was no question about it now—the gargoyle was alive!

Derek still felt frozen in place. The gargoyle was no more than twenty feet away. Derek saw the creature turn and stare at him. Then the gargoyle suddenly moved into the shadows.

Derek knew the gargoyle was hiding, but he couldn't see where. Then a third flash of lightning hit the garden. Derek saw the gargoyle creeping toward him. He could see its awful, grinning face.

Finally, Derek willed himself to move. He started to run for the house. But he felt as if he were moving in slow motion, as if he were in a dream.

As Derek reached the doors in front of his bedroom, he turned his head. He could see the gargoyle in the light coming from the garden. The creature was only a few feet behind him!

He grabbed for the doorknobs. But the doors wouldn't open. He looked around frantically. Maybe he could make a run for his uncle's bedroom.

But the gargoyle seemed to guess what he was thinking. It cut across the lawn and placed itself between Derek and his uncle's bedroom.

Derek felt as if he were out of his mind with fear. He couldn't think.

He had no choice. He had to run back into the garden. His feet felt as if they were made of lead. His heart was thumping wildly. He could hear the gargoyle following him. But he wasn't brave enough to look behind.

Then the garden lights went out. Derek guessed it was because of the storm. He ran through the dark garden. Suddenly he tripped. He fell by the base of another statue.

Derek started to get up. He looked around, but he couldn't see a thing.

There was a crash of thunder. Derek felt the first drops of rain fall against his hot face.

As he hurried to his feet, lightning flashed again. Derek saw the gargoyle on its back legs only a few yards away from him. It was getting ready to spring!

He cried out and fell against the base of the statue next to him. Just then he heard a sound, like a guitar string being plucked. A second later he heard a howl of rage and pain and the sound of footsteps running away.

In the quiet that followed, Derek lay against the base of the statue. He couldn't move or even think.

Then he heard a noise behind the bushes. He guessed it was the gargoyle coming back.

But when a dark figure came out from the bushes, he saw it was his uncle Tobias. He had a large flashlight in his hands.

"Derek!" he cried as he noticed the young boy lying on the ground. "Are you okay? What are you doing out here?"

Derek opened his mouth to speak but nothing came out.

"I thought I heard someone screaming," his uncle said as he helped Derek to his feet. "Was that you?"

Derek could only shake his head and point in the direction that the howling scream had come from.

His uncle shone the flashlight and gasped as he saw the statue of the gargoyle lying on the ground. Derek watched his uncle walk over to it. But he couldn't bring himself to follow.

Uncle Tobias came back, shaking his head slowly. "It's the darndest thing I ever saw," he said. "A lightning bolt must have knocked the gargoyle off its base."

Derek just nodded.

"But that's not the strangest thing," Derek's uncle went on. "It has an arrow right through its chest!"

Then Uncle Tobias shone the light up at the statue under which Derek had been huddled. He cried, "Well I'll be . . ."

Derek looked up, too. It was the statue of the

goddess. It looked the same as it had that afternoon—except for one thing. The bowstring was loose and the arrow was gone!

Now Derek finally found his voice.

"It—*she* killed the gargoyle," he said.

"*Killed* the gargoyle?" his uncle repeated.

Derek nodded. How could he tell his uncle all that had really happened? He couldn't believe it himself.

"It's true," he finally blurted.

His uncle looked down on him kindly and then up again at the goddess.

"Come on," he said. "Let's go inside and have some milk and cake. I want to know everything that happened—right from the beginning. I've seen some strange things in my travels. But this may turn out to be the strangest."

Derek slowly followed his uncle back to the house. But just before he went in, he turned around and looked toward the archer.

"Thank you," he whispered as thunder rolled across the sky and a heavy rain began to fall.

The Mummy's Hand

MY DOG, BOOMER, is stupid. There's no other word for it. I mean, I love him and all that. But he just isn't too bright. He's half beagle and half cocker spaniel. Those kinds of dogs are pretty smart. But I guess he got the wrong half of each one.

I had been trying to teach him an easy trick for two weeks. He still hadn't gotten the hang of it.

All I wanted him to do was fetch a stick or ball when I threw it. I tried throwing something, pointing to it, and saying "Fetch!" But he would just look at me and wag his tail.

Then I tried "Get!" That almost worked. At least Boomer would run over to what I pointed at. He'd sniff it. But he wouldn't bring it back to me.

I'd just about given up. But I kept on trying

the trick with him every day anyway. I figured that sooner or later, he might get the idea.

This afternoon I was walking by a pet store. I saw a big red rubber bone in the window. Boomer likes bones. So I got an idea. Maybe if I bought him the bone he would finally learn the trick.

My birthday had been three days before. My parents had given me twenty-five dollars. I had the money in my pocket, so I went into the store. I paid five dollars for the bone. I was heading home, when I noticed this little shop a few blocks down from the pet store. It was one of those dusty old stores that sell weird things from all over the world. I stopped to look in the window. I saw an old skull, some strange-looking pots, and a sharp knife with a snake on its handle. There were all kinds of things I didn't even know the names of.

I love weird things. I always have. Years ago when kids my age were watching silly cartoons, I would be watching horror movies. And my favorite stories are about strange things that happen all around the world.

Anyway, as I was looking in the window, I saw

something wonderful. I walked into the store. I said to the tall, thin man who was working there, "Is that a mummy's hand in the window?"

The man looked at the hand and then answered, "Sure enough, kid. I just got it in the other day. Some old geezer sold it to me. He sure seemed glad to get rid of it, too. He was mumbling something about it being cursed."

I thought the guy was kidding. He had a funny little smile on his face. Even though I like horror movies, I really don't believe in curses.

So I just asked, "How much is it?"

I'd guessed it would cost too much for me.

The thin guy raised his eyebrows and said, "You want to buy it?"

I nodded. I could swear he looked relieved.

"But I only have ten dollars to spend," I added. Mummy's hand or not, I didn't want to spend *all* my money on it.

The man smiled and said, "Why, that's exactly what I'm asking for it."

Without another word, he went over to the window and picked up the hand. And as he brought it over, he held it out as if it were a live lobster. He looked really scared of the hand.

He put it in a bag for me and took my ten dollars. I left the store with the hand in my hand.

As soon as I got home, I ran up to my room.

We live in a big old house, and my room is in the attic. My mom and dad let me fix it up the way I wanted. It is as far from their own bedroom as it can be. I feel as if I have my own world.

Anyway, as soon as I got in my room, I put the mummy's hand on a shelf across the room from my bed. Then I went over to my bed and started to take off my sneakers. Just then, my dog, Boomer, came into the room.

"Hey, I almost forgot," I said. "I have a present for you."

I took out the bone I had bought. Boomer sniffed it and wagged his tail.

"Good dog," I said. "You like the bone?"

Then I threw it across the room near my shelves and said, "Get, get!"

Boomer went over to the bone with his big tongue hanging out. He sniffed it again.

"That's it," I said. "Now get it, get it."

First Boomer looked at me. Then he looked

down at the bone. Finally he plopped down and started to chew on it.

I shook my head. My dumb dog was *never* going to learn the trick.

Just before bedtime, I was in my room, watching a horror movie on TV. It was just about over, when my dad called from downstairs, "It's almost bedtime."

"Sure, Dad," I yelled back. "I'll go to sleep in a minute. Right after the movie's over."

I heard my dad walk back into the den. Just then I happened to look up at the mummy's hand on my shelf. The only light in the room was coming from the TV set. In the flickering glow, I thought I saw the hand twitch.

I looked again. But it didn't move anymore.

I shrugged. It must have been a trick of the light, I thought. As soon as the movie was over, I got into my bed and pulled the blankets up and closed my eyes.

Suddenly I woke up. I looked at the big white alarm clock next to my bed. It was only two o'clock in the morning.

I was about to close my eyes again when I heard a strange noise. It sounded as if a squirrel or some other small animal was in my room.

For a second I thought it was Boomer. But I looked and saw him sleeping peacefully in his usual spot by my feet.

I heard the noise again, and I sat up. The moonlight streaming through the large windows made everything look ghostly. I could make out the shelf where I put the mummy's hand. It was gone!

Then I heard the noise again. It sounded closer than before. I sat up straighter. Something that looked like a big spider or large crab moved across the wooden floor of my room. It was heading right for my bed!

As the thing came closer, I could see it better.

It *wasn't* a spider or a crab. It was the mummy's hand!

I was so scared that I started to shake. Suddenly I heard myself cry out softly.

Maybe the mummy's hand *did* have a curse on it, as the store owner had said. Maybe the thing was alive!

I knew I wasn't dreaming. I shook so hard that the bed creaked. This woke Boomer up. Instead of growling and barking, my dumb dog just stared at the creeping hand. For all the good that did, he could have stayed asleep.

I couldn't seem to move my body. I just stared as the hand crept closer and closer.

The thing was now about halfway across the room and still getting closer. I shuddered. I couldn't take it anymore.

I looked at Boomer. He was my last hope. "G- get it!" I stammered. "Get—get it *away*."

Boomer raised one long ear and looked at me. Then he looked at the hand. He jumped off the bed.

I sighed in relief. Boomer was finally going to do something. Then I had realized what I had said—"Get it."

"No!" I cried out. "Boomer, don't!"

Too late. Boomer was already picking up the creepy-looking thing in his mouth.

I watched in horror. Boomer wagged his tail and moved toward me with the twitching hand in his mouth. The clawlike fingers opened and

closed as if they were trying to grab something.

Suddenly Boomer bounded up onto my bed. The hand was still in his mouth. As Boomer came closer, the fingers reached out for me. "Oh, no," I managed to croak, still unable to move. "*Now* you learned how to do the trick!"

Trick or Treat

JESSIE STARED AT the witch's mask that her best friend, Hillary, was holding up. Jessie's eyes grew wide. It was like no other mask she had ever seen. As she stared harder, a small shiver ran up her spine.

The mask looked almost like real skin. Jessie could even see tiny wrinkles around the nose, the mouth, and the eyes. And there was a dark mole on one cheek, with tiny hairs sticking out of it.

"It's perfect, isn't it?" Hillary asked.

"It's scary-looking!" Jessie answered.

Jessie and Hillary had been looking through a box of old masks. They had stopped into Twice Born, a used-clothing store, on the way home from school. They were going to a Halloween party the next night.

The girls had waited almost until the last minute to decide on their costumes. They just hadn't come up with anything special enough to suit them. They had thought Twice Born might have something they could wear.

They had looked at everything. But nothing had seemed quite right. Then the owner, an old man with thin white hair and a long sharp nose, had snapped his fingers.

"I almost forgot," he had said. "I got in a box of old masks the other day." He had flashed a smile that was missing a few teeth.

"I got the masks from a magic shop that closed. They're in the back corner of the store. You're welcome to look through them if you like.

"Three dollars each, if you're interested," he had added.

Jessie and Hillary had thought that the masks were a great idea. They had lost no time in going to the box and pulling out masks.

A few minutes later, Hillary had found the witch's mask.

"I-I really don't like that mask," Jessie said.

34

Hillary looked hurt, then angry. But soon she smiled brightly.

"Well, I *do* like it," she said. "And I'm going to buy it."

"I wish you wouldn't," said Jessie.

"Why not?" asked Hillary. "The way you're going on, you'd think it was real. Now, stop. I want it."

Jessie still wished Hillary would change her mind. But she told herself, "You're being silly. It's just an old mask."

"Now we have to get *you* a mask," Hillary said. "Here's one." Hillary held up a clown's mask.

Jessie shook her head. "I'll see what's at the bottom of the box," she said. She reached down into the pile of masks.

"Oh, I'm sure there's nothing better there," said Hillary.

"How would you know?" asked Jessie as she kept looking.

Hillary shrugged and pressed her lips tightly together.

Jessie gave her friend a strange look. She returned to the box. Suddenly she noticed a beautiful face staring up at her from the bottom.

It was the mask of a fairy princess, as beautiful as the witch's mask was ugly.

"This is great!" she cried as she lifted the mask up and showed it to Hillary. "It's just what I wanted."

Like the witch's mask, the soft smooth skin looked real. There was even a hint of pink on each cheek. The straight thin nose and soft round mouth were beautifully shaped, as if an artist had spent hours painting the face.

Hillary stared at the mask. She had a strange look on her face. Then she said in a mocking voice, "Why, it's the Good Fairy!"

The way Hillary looked and sounded made Jessie feel creepy. "What's the matter with you?" Jessie asked.

Hillary's eyes met Jessie's and blinked. Suddenly she smiled like the Hillary that Jessie knew.

"Nothing's the matter. I'm fine. I really am."

Hillary looked back at the Good Fairy mask. Then she held up the witch's mask.

"That's funny," she said. "These two masks

look very different from all the rest. They're much more like real faces."

Jessie looked down at the rest of the masks in the box. It was true. All the other masks were made of paper or cloth. But the two they held seemed almost to have a life of their own.

"Maybe these masks cost more, too," Jessie whispered in Hillary's ear.

Just then the old man came back.

"Found anything you like, kids?"

Hillary and Jessie held up their masks and nodded.

"How much are these?" asked Jessie.

"Same as the others—three dollars each."

"Oh, they looked like they would cost more," said Jessie honestly.

Hillary gave her a poke in the side.

Jessie looked at her friend in surprise. She knew Hillary was just as honest as she was.

"Well, miss, it's real nice of you to point that out, but I never change my price. I said the masks were three dollars each, and that's what they are."

The girls gave their money to the old man.

They left the store with their masks in brown-paper bags.

On the way home, they talked about what clothes to wear with their masks.

"I can wear my mother's long black dress and her black shawl," Hillary said. "That would be real witchy-looking."

"Great," agreed Jessie. "And I have that long white dress I wore in the class play last year when I was the Snow Queen. That's exactly what the Good Fairy would wear.

"I can't wait until the party tomorrow night," Jessie added. "We're going to have the best costumes."

"Yes, I'll be the bad old witch, and you'll be the good sweet fairy," Hillary said with an odd smile. "There's a saying that opposites attract, right?"

The next night was Halloween. It was clear and cold. The two friends walked quickly to keep themselves warm. They were dressed just as they had decided the day before.

The party was being held at a house at the other end of the road on which they both lived.

There were a number of houses along the half mile, but they were all set back from the road and partly hidden by tall trees. Even though the road was dark and empty, the girls both felt safe in their own neighborhood.

But as Jessie walked along, she looked down at her Good Fairy mask and couldn't help feeling uneasy. When she had stopped for her friend, Hillary already had her mask on. But she had asked Jessie not to wear hers.

Jessie had thought it was a strange thing to ask. But Hillary had said that she couldn't see very well through her mask and had asked the Good Fairy to lead the way for her.

As the girls walked along, they came to the only part of the road they didn't like. It passed by a small, boarded-up church. Next door was an old graveyard.

Jessie could see the tombstones. They looked like big crooked teeth sticking up from the ground. She shivered and waited for Hillary to say something. Hillary had always hated to pass the graveyard, too. But she had been strangely quiet since they had left her house.

A full moon suddenly peeked out from behind

the church. In the light, Hillary's mask seemed to be more real than ever.

As Jessie stared at her, she realized she was looking *up* at her friend. She *knew* they were both the same height. But now Hillary was at least two inches taller.

Jessie was about to say something when Hillary hissed, "Oh, look, a little cemetery off all by itself."

Then Hillary mumbled some words in a language that Jessie had never heard before. As she finished, she turned to Jessie and smiled. Jessie's back stiffened. There was something wrong.

Then she understood. It wasn't Hillary who had smiled. It was the mask!

"Let's go see if any of my friends are buried there," Hillary suddenly whispered. Her voice sounded low and rough, as if she had a cold.

What is she talking about? Jessie wondered.

Suddenly Hillary turned her face up toward the moon. Jessie watched with fear as Hillary let out a low howl, like a wolf. Then Hillary stared at Jessie.

Now it was clear to Jessie. Somehow, the mask had turned Hillary into a *real witch*!

Jessie gathered all her courage and yelled, "What have you done to my friend?"

The witch smiled. "You have a strong life force," she said. She pointed a crooked finger at Jessie. "That is the one thing I need to bring me back to my full power."

She grabbed Jessie by the arms. The mask almost fell out of Jessie's hand.

"Give me that thing!" the witch growled. "I know what to do with goody-goodies like you!"

Jessie couldn't explain to herself what was going on. But she didn't care. She just knew she had to get away from the witch, no matter what.

She broke free of the witch's grasp and ran across the road toward the graveyard. She could hear the witch screaming for her to stop. But she kept on running.

When Jessie reached the graveyard, she hesitated. But the graveyard scared her less than the "thing" she was trying to escape.

Without waiting another second, she raced through the graveyard, zigzagging between the tombstones. She could see the dark, deserted church to her right. It seemed to mock her as she ran by.

Jessie stumbled to the other end of the grave-yard. A thick row of bushes blocked her path. She squeezed through them, only to find a stone wall behind them too high to climb. She was trapped!

She spun around. Her body trembled. She wanted to run, but she didn't know what good it would do. The witch had to be close behind her.

With a terrible feeling of dread, she crawled back through the bushes and hid behind a large tombstone. Her heart was beating wildly. Her breath came in short gasps.

She tried to stop her hands from shaking. It was then that she saw she was still clutching the Good Fairy mask.

"I wonder what would happen if I put this on?" Jessie asked herself. "Would I turn into a good fairy?"

Suddenly she heard the witch's mean laugh nearby. Jessie lifted her head and saw the awful face of the witch staring down at her from over the top of the tombstone.

"Peek-a-boo!" the witch hissed.

Jessie gasped and, with shaking fingers, put on her mask. She heard the witch suck in her breath as if someone had hit her.

Then a warm feeling spread over Jessie's whole body. It was as if the sun had come out in the middle of the night.

With the mask on, Jessie was no longer afraid. She rose from her hiding place and faced the witch.

Jessie felt her mouth open, but the voice that came out was not her own. "Once more you have tried to beat me, Wicked One," she heard the voice say sweetly but strongly. "You know your power is strongest on Halloween night. But you forget that wherever you go, I shall follow. Good will always conquer evil."

Quickly, as if it had a mind of its own, her hand tugged at the witch's face.

"Oh!" screamed the witch. "Your touch of goodness burns me!"

Jessie ripped off the witch's mask and threw it to the ground. Then Jessie looked up. There was the old Hillary standing before her, looking dazed.

Jessie took off her own mask and let it fall to

the ground. Slowly she went over to her friend and put her arm around her shoulder.

"Are you okay?" she asked.

Hillary nodded as she looked down at the two masks lying side by side on the ground. And as they watched, the witch's mask shriveled, cracked, and finally disappeared in a puff of black smoke. The Good Fairy mask glowed. Then it disappeared in a flash of bright-blue light. Soon afterward, a sweet smell filled the air.

For a few minutes, the two friends stared at the ground where the masks had been. Then they turned toward each other.

"What happened?" Hillary finally asked. She hid her face in her hands and started to cry.

"You turned into a witch," Jessie whispered. "But it wasn't really you. It was the mask.

"You're not *really* a witch," she added.

Hillary took her hands away and stared at Jessie.

"And I'm not really the Good Fairy," said Jessie.

The two of them were quiet once more. Neither one knew what else to say.

Then Hillary seemed to get control of herself. "Let's not let a mean old witch mess up our Halloween," she said, sounding like the old Hillary. "We can still have a good time at the party even if we don't really have our whole costumes anymore."

"Yeah," said Jessie, quickly feeling better. "I guess we'll just have to go as ourselves."

"I can't think of two nicer people," said Hillary.

"Neither can I," said Jessie.

Creature Feature

ERIC CLICKED THROUGH the channels on the TV set. There wasn't a good picture on any of them. Eric's house was far from the nearest town, and cable hadn't arrived yet. His parents had laughed when he had asked if they could buy a satellite dish.

Now, with a storm coming, the picture was even worse than usual. Eric could hear the low moan of the wind as it shook the bare branches of the trees along the road leading to town.

He was baby-sitting his five-year-old brother, Billy, while his parents went to a movie. He didn't mind looking after Billy. But he did mind living so far from town.

He often asked himself, "What if something happens and I need help in a hurry?"

Then he shrugged. Everything was fine, and

nothing was going to happen. Billy had gone to bed an hour ago. Eric had just finished making some popcorn. And now all he needed was a good movie on TV.

But the old set was showing only fuzzy stripes. Eric was about to give up when suddenly a channel came in bright and clear. He looked to see which channel it was. The dial was stuck between two channels.

Well, it's a clear picture, Eric thought. I might as well leave it on.

The wind kept moaning as he settled into the soft chair in front of the TV. He dug into the bowl of popcorn he had placed on the small table in front of him.

At that second a movie started on the TV. It looked like it was going to be one of those scary creature movies.

The opening scene was a small, lonely-looking cemetery. The music told Eric that something strange would happen any minute. He stared at the screen. . . .

The gate of the old cemetery was rusted and worn. Statues on either side of it had pieces broken off.

In front, patches of brown, dried-up grass covered the cold-looking earth.

The tombstones were all leaning toward each other. It was as if they were trying to keep warm.

Something about the movie seemed familiar to Eric. But he didn't know what. Maybe I've seen this before, he thought.

There was a whisper of movement under one of the tombstones. It was as if the earth were breathing. Suddenly the ground cracked. Something was trying to get out.

Two bony arms pushed themselves through a wide crack in the earth. A head popped up, grinning like a horrible jack-in-the-box.

A hideous creature that had once been a man pulled itself out of the ground. With eyes that were no more than holes, it looked straight ahead. Then it began to walk away.

Suddenly, other dead creatures popped out of the ground. They followed the first creature out of the cemetery. They walked in a line as the wind blew the torn pieces of cloth that used to be their clothes.

Lightning flashed through the night sky. Up

49

the road, a small town could be seen. Rain was starting to fall.

Eric jumped in his seat as he heard the sound of rain outside. He felt strange.

He wondered whether or not he should change channels. But he couldn't take his eyes off the movie. There was something so real about the dead creatures.

"What a makeup job!" he said to himself. And he continued watching.

Now the creatures from the cemetery neared a house on the road to town. And as they did, they growled and screamed and pointed. Then three of them started toward the house.

Eric stared at the TV. It felt as if hundreds of tiny pins were sticking into his body. Now he knew why the movie looked familiar.

The cemetery that the creatures had come out of was the old one a few miles down the road. The town was the nearby town. The road they were traveling along was the road outside. And the house the three creatures were headed for was *his* house!

Now Eric could hear other sounds outside

above the wind. There were growls and screams, exactly like the ones the creatures in the movie were making.

He kept staring at the TV. His body froze as the movie went on.

The three creatures came closer to the house. The others kept on parading up the road.

A light could be seen in the front window of the house. It was a small ghostly light, as if someone were watching TV.

The biggest creature smiled, showing long yellow teeth. He moved slowly. But he seemed to know where he was going. The two other creatures were the remains of what had once been a man and a woman. They marched slowly behind him with the same measured step.

Now the creature in front walked onto the porch of the house.

Eric was still unable to move. He could hear the heavy thump of feet on the porch outside. Part of him wanted to look out the window and prove that nothing was there. But another part of him didn't have the courage.

"There *couldn't* be anything outside," he told himself. "I'm only watching a horror movie. In real life, dead people don't pop out of the ground and walk the earth. Anyway, I locked the front and back doors—didn't I?"

Suddenly Eric wasn't sure. And he still couldn't bring himself to look out the window. The only thing he could look at was the picture on the TV. . . .

The first of the terrible-looking creatures reached the front door. He started to pound slowly and heavily on it. One, two, three times.

Eric heard the same sound against his door at almost the same time. He jumped. Now he knew his fears were coming true. Somehow everything that was happening in the movie was really happening.

He felt all alone. What could he do? How could he fight these creatures?

Then a thought came to him so quickly that it made him smile.

He could turn off the TV! That was it. Maybe if he turned the movie off, the creatures would go away.

He tried to stand but he couldn't. He felt as if he were glued to the chair. The movie went on.

The creature who had been pounding was now

trying to open the front door. The two other creatures stood behind him, grinning horribly.

That was enough to send Eric jumping up from the chair. He stumbled against the table, spilling the popcorn all over the floor. He heard the door suddenly swing wide open.

It *hadn't* been locked. Or if it had been, it hadn't made any difference to the things on the porch. With his heart pounding, Eric raced to the TV.

Now the first creature was halfway through the door. The other two were close behind. Suddenly they all started to growl and scream.

As Eric reached the TV, an awful smell filled the air. It was as if something long dead had been uncovered. He tried to turn the TV off. But his hands were slippery with sweat.

"Come on, come on," he told himself as the creatures kept up their terrible cries from the hall.

To his horror, the TV picture showed that the creatures were no more than a few feet away from the living room.

Finally Eric just hit the switch with his hand, and the TV clicked off. With that, the smell suddenly went away. The only sounds he heard were the wind and rain as they beat against the house.

Eric's idea had worked. It was over. He staggered over to the chair and fell into it.

He was just starting to breathe a little more easily when he suddenly felt a hand grab his shoulder.

He sat right up and swung his head around in wide-eyed fear.

It was only Billy, a sleepy look on his five-year-old face.

"The front door was open," the little boy said. "But I locked it. Daddy and Mommy said we should."

Eric nodded, and for a second he couldn't say a word. When he finally got his voice back, he muttered, "What are you doing out of bed?"

"I couldn't sleep," answered Billy. "I heard some funny noises down here."

Eric hugged his brother in a rush of relief. He did not want to tell Billy the terrible truth.

"I was just watching some dumb old horror movie," Eric said. "But I turned it off."

Billy nodded and then smiled.

"Can I stay down here with you? I don't like the lightning and thunder."

Eric smiled back at his little brother and said, "Okay, but only if we don't watch TV."